MORAL STORIES

Best Moral Stories for children

SUMAIYYA JAGIRDAR

ISBN 978-93-5559-224-8
© SUMAIYYA JAGIRDAR 2021
Published in India 2021 by Pencil

A brand of
One Point Six Technologies Pvt. Ltd.
123, Building J2, Shram Seva Premises,
Wadala Truck Terminal, Wadala (E)
Mumbai 400037, Maharashtra, INDIA
E connect@thepencilapp.com
W www.thepencilapp.com

DISCLAIMER: *This is a work of fiction. Names, characters, places, events and incidents are the products of the author's imagination. The opinions expressed in this book do not seek to reflect the views of the Publisher.*

Author biography

Sumaiyya Jagirdar was born on 9th March, By profession, she is a software engineer and loves to write and to do other creative things like painting, sketching, crafting, henna designing, etc, she is the founder of SN Graphics and Henna Design World.

CONTENTS

Epigraph

A child is a uncut diamond

-Austin Omalley

Foreword

Stories in this book are very simple and easy, if a parent is narrating the story to a child at night, you can make your child fall asleep soon and fall into good dreams, after children read or hear moral stories they start implementing the good things in their life.

Acknowledgements

All stories are written by the author, referring to the stories that she heard being a child from her ancestors, stories are fiction and are written intending to make a child understand the life moral in a creative way.

Introduction

This book has a collection of the moral stories written by the author intending to make children understand the moral value sof the life by along with reading, making a child understand the life lessions in a formal way is little difficult so the book consists of the creative and entertaining stories which create curiosity in children to understand what happens in the story.

Arrogant King

There was once a king. He was very arrogant with his kingdom's citizens; when they came to him for help, he used to speak rudely, insult them, and send them away without listening to their problems.

One day, an elderly woman prayed to God, requesting that a fairy be sent to teach this king a proper lesson.

Queen gave birth to princes, The princess was very beautiful, she grew up to be 8 years old, but she couldn't talk.

The king and queen were distraught over their daughter's condition; many doctors came from all over to treat her, but no one could get her to speak.

One fine day, the king and queen sat in the garden under a tree, and the queen was crying, "Why can't my daughter talk?" She questioned God's existence.

A white fairy appeared with a magic stick, saying, "Your daughter cannot speak because of your husband."

But how exactly? Queen inquired.

Your husband is arrogant and rude to the people of your kingdom when they come to him for help; they are unhappy, and your daughter is unable to speak as a result.

Oh! God! Please assist me; I am deeply ashamed of my actions; and please assist me in making my daughter talk. The king said to the fairy.

You must go to every home in your kingdom and apologize to the people of your kingdom for being arrogant and rude to them, listen to their problems, and solve them until every citizen of your kingdom forgives you, said the fairy.

The king went to every house and apologized for his behavior, and the princess began to speak.

Moral: Do not hurt, anyone, with your behavior.

Liar Boy

One day, a boy and his sister went to a picnic from school; all of the children were enjoying their visit to the zoo, and teachers were keeping an eye on all of the children to ensure their safety.

While playing in a zoo, a boy began screaming, the lion's cage broke, and a lion emerged; everyone present became terrified and fled to a safe location.

Hahaha, I was joking, said the boy, to which everyone became enraged and the school staff scolded him.

Stop lying in everything; if you keep doing it, no one will come to your aid when you are in real danger, said his sister.

I keep joking, and lying is fun. It was a funny prank, and I enjoyed seeing how everyone in the zoo got scared and started screaming here and there.

Now it seems fun to you, but when you're in a really bad situation and need help, no one will believe you, and you'll realize how damaging a lie can be, said his sister.

Everyone in the zoo resumed their enjoyment of the zoo, and the boy and his friend were climbing a tree when the boy suddenly fell from a height, began crying in pain, and begged for help, but this time everyone in the zoo dismissed it as a prank.

The boy sobbed to his sister, "I fell from a great height, I was hurt, and none of you came to help," he explained.

I've already told you not to prank on everything; see, when you needed help, no one came to you because you've left a bad impression on people.

Moral: Never, ever lie.

Greedy Girl

Sara and Nancy, two friends in a class. They were good friends who shared everything, they were both bright students in the class.

Tara had a secret magical pencil box that never ran out of pencils. Every day, she took a new pencil from the pencil box. Tara also gave a lot of pencils to her friend Nancy and other classmates.

How do you bring a new pencil every day? Don't your parents tell you not to buy so many pencils? Nancy inquired. I don't buy them; I get them through magic, don't ask how. Tara explained, "I can't tell you because it's a secret."

Nancy was in tara's house for a school project one day, and out of curiosity, she asked tara's mom about the pencils she brings to school every day.

No, we don't buy her so many pencils, said tara's mother, she brings new pencils to school every day, she has a few pencils of different colors, and you might be confused.

Nancy was curious as to how tara brought so many pencils, so she began spying on her, and one day she discovered that it is a magic box from which tara receives new pencils every day.

Nancy intended to steal it from Tara so that she could have new pencils every day as well. Nancy, on the other hand, was unaware that stealing the box from Tara would result in its destruction with magic.

Nancy finally stole the box from Tara and put it in her bag, then went home happy that she would now get new pencils every day. She took out the box and placed it on the table.

The box turned to ash and vanished, and no one will ever receive new pencils again.

The moral of the story is that greed is bad.

Helping Hand

There was a small town and people of that town were reserved people, they never botheredabout their neighbors, not interested in doing any good work, nor they were doing any bad to anyone.

Among them there was one person who was a thief, he stole many things from severalrich people of that town.

By the end of the day he used to visit poor people and help them by giving them food and money.

One fine day a Goddess appeared in that town, all people gathered wondering about the appearance of the goddess.

I am here to bless with wealth and health to the people who do good work by helping the needy, feeding hungry, etc, and punish one who does bad works.

All people thought that goddesses will punish that bad thief who steals money and costly things from rich people.

She checked the whole town, and she blessed the thief with wealth and health, that thief now became the richest person in the town.

He is a thief, steals money and other costly things from rich people. Why do you bless him with wealth? Asked people to the goddess.

Of course, he stole the things from you all but he helped the poor and needy, he fed food to hungry with that money, stealing is a bad thing but his good deeds overpowered his bad things, now that he is wealthy he will not steal hereafter and keep helping the poor.

Moral: Keep doing good things, you will be blessed.

Everyone is special

Once, a boy came home from school crying because he had failed to win the long jump competition, while his friend had won the prize.

His mother took him to the zoo on the second day and showed him all of the animals and asked him to carefully observe them.

"Did you notice the elephant? what was it doing?" mother inquired while returning home. "Elephant was so big, and because it was heavy, it was a little slow compared to other animals, but it could easily lift heavy wood," the boy replied.

How was the monkey behaving? Mom inquired. "I saw a group of so many monkeys in the zoo, and they were all active and jumping from one place to another," the boy replied.

How was Peacock? Mother inquired, and the boy replied, "The peacock is beautiful, and it was dancing, opening its feathers wide."

All animals in the zoo have their specialties; elephants cannot dance like peacocks, cannot jump like monkeys, but can lift heavy objects, and monkeys and peacocks cannot lift heavy objects like elephants and. God made everyone unique, each with their own set of skills.

When someone else outperforms you in something, don't get upset. Perhaps you are talented in another area.

Moral: Everyone is a special

Jumping Frogs

Once, a group of frogs was playing in the ground, and two of them fell into a pit by mistake.

Both frogs began jumping to get out of the pit, while all other frogs outside the pit yelled, "there is no way to escape from the pit, you are badly stuck under the pit."

One of the frogs became tired and sat outside the pit listening to the other frogs, but the other frog kept jumping and eventually jumped so high that he escaped the pit.

The rest of the frogs were astounded to see that frog make it out of the pit and the frog that escaped from the pit was deaf, the frog mistook all the frogs who were encouraging him to come out of the pit and kept jumping until he succeeded. another frog got affected by the demotivation of the frogs outside and stopped jumping.

Moral: Have faith in yourself and never let the opinions of others influence you.

Circus Elephants

Once upon a time in a circus, the ringmaster tied six elephants with a weak rope each, that they could easily break and escape from, but none of the elephants even tried to break that rope.

A visitor asked the ringmaster, "Why did you tie those elephants with such a weak rope? Elephants are so big and strong that they can easily break the rope and escape."

The elephants were led to believe that they were too weak to break the ropes and escape, according to the ringmaster. They didn't even try to break the ropes now because of this belief.

Elephants don't even try to break the rope because they are made to believe that they are too weak to break the rope.

Moral: Don't limit to societal constraints. Believe that you can accomplish anything you set your mind to!

Gold Greedy

Once upon a time, in a small town, there lived a man who was a carpenter and a hard worker who happily lived with his wife and two children.

On his way to the market one day, he noticed an elderly woman struggling to cross the road, so he assisted her.

That old woman transformed into a fairy and was so moved by the man's gesture that she offered him a wish that she could grant.

The man requested that a fairy bestows upon him the ability to turn everything he touches into gold.

The fairy told him that while she could grant his wish, but gold is not happiness, and the more he used this power, the more unhappy he became with it.

The fairy granted him his wish and then vanished. The man was overjoyed and went back to his house, where he began touching everything in the house and they all turned to gold.

With excitement, he touched his wife and children, who also turned into gold statues; however, seeing his family as lifeless statues, he became sad.

He now realized that the fairy had warned him that the more he used his power, the more unhappy he would become.

The man returned to the same location in search of the fairy, but he couldn't find her, so he sat under the tree tired.

The fairy appeared, and the man explained his problem to her. The fairy then said I will grant you one more wish "What do you want?"

The man begged the fairy to give him his family back alive, make him more hardworking, and bless him to keep his wife and children happy.

Moral: Don't be greedy when you get something.

Ice Cream Seller

Once upon a time, brother and sister were sitting ice cream in a garden on a bench, there comes an Ice cream seller.

Sister wanted to eat ice cream but her brother told her we do not have money so we are not buying it.

The ice cream seller heard them and offered free ice cream but the brother denied taking it stating that the ice cream seller is a stranger and our parents are not in the garden right now so taking something from strangers is not good.

but the ice cream was very tempting so the sister couldn't resist herself so she took it and ate it, and the ice-cream seller was convincing her to come along with him, he will give more ice cream to her.

Seeing that brother felt there is something fishy so he went to his sister, as he approaches his sister, she started feeling dizzy, with the presence of mind boy screamed for help, people gathered and rescued the girl from the ice-cream seller.

Moral: Never take anything from the stranger

Who Is Obedient

Once upon a time, a father had two sons, and one fine day while walking to the office, he called both sons in the hall and asked the young son Steve to water the plants in the balcony, but Steve refused and argued with his father, saying I am going to my friend's house to play cricket, so I can't water, and in anger ran to his room.

Father instructed his eldest son John to water the plants; John bowed his head and agreed to water the plants; father complimented him, saying "Good boy," and then left for the office.

After his father left for work, John turned on the television and sat on the sofa the whole day watching TV, without watering the plants.

After 30 minutes, Steve realized that his behavior toward his father was inappropriate, so he watered the plants, and went to his friends' house to play cricket.

Activity: Share this with your friends and family and get to know according to them who is obedient?

Write your answer in the box given below

Glossary

Arrogant: very worried and upset. unpleasantly proud and behaving as if you are more important than, or know more than, other people

Distraught: very worried and upset.

Terrified: cause to feel extreme fear.

Enraged: very angry; furious.

Emerge: move out of or away from something and become visible.

Prank: a practical joke or mischievous act.

Impression: an idea, feeling, or opinion about something or someone, especially one formed without conscious thought or on the basis of little evidence.

Curiosity: a strong desire to know or learn something.

Destruction: the action or process of causing so much damage to something that it no longer exists or cannot be repaired.

Notes

Let your children write a story of there own imagination